The Unicorns of Blossom Wood

Scholastic Children's Books
An imprint of Scholastic Ltd
Euston House, 24 Eversholt Street,
London, NW1 1DB, UK
Registered office: Westfield Road, Southam, Warwickshire, CV47 0RA
SCHOLASTIC and associated logos are trademarks and/or registered
trademarks of Scholastic Inc.

First published in the UK by Scholastic Ltd, 2017

ISBN 978 1407 17124 1

A CIP catalogue record for this book is available from the British Library.

Printed by CPI Group (UK) Ltd, Croydon, CR0 4YY
Papers used by Scholastic Children's Books are made
from wood grown in sustainable forests.

1 3 5 7 9 10 8 6 4 2

This is a work of fiction. Names, characters, places, incidents
and dialogues are products of the author's imagination or are used
fictitiously. Any resemblance to actual people, living or dead,
events or locales is entirely coincidental.

www.scholastic.co.uk

Catherine Coe

Unicorn games & quizzes inside!

The Unicorns of Blossom Wood

Storms and Rainbows

SCHOLASTIC

For the fan-doobly-tastic Lucy Rogers.
Thank you for all the passion and editorial magic
you've brought to Blossom Wood xxx

Thanks to Dina von Lowenkraft for all your
invaluable advice and suggestions.

Chapter 1
Looking for Lei

"Where's Lei?" Cora asked her cousin Isabelle. Lei had been walking on the gravel path beside them minutes ago, but now Cora could only see their parents up ahead. They all had binoculars pressed to their eyes as they searched for birds in the blue sky.

Isabelle stopped and spun around. "Did

we leave her behind?" she replied, but
she could only see Lei's older sister, Ying,
nodding her bright pink hair to the
music coming through her earbuds.

Cora readjusted the heart hairclip
in her blonde bob as she thought for
a moment. "Maybe she's somewhere
collecting science stuff. She brought those

plastic tubs along for our nature walk, didn't she?"

They scanned the valley around them. Soon Isabelle spotted a patch of brown hair poking up behind an old stone wall. She nudged Cora and pointed, and the two of them began running across the grass.

They climbed over the wall and found Lei sitting behind it, her arms wrapped around her legs. She didn't look like she was finding things for her science project – her rucksack was still on her back and she was staring straight ahead, scowling.

"Lei! What are you doing?" asked Isabelle.

Lei turned her big brown eyes to her cousins for a second, then went back to staring again. "Nothing!"

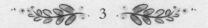

Cora shuffled down beside her. "It doesn't look like nothing," she said gently. "Are you angry with us?"

Lei let out a sigh and shook her head. "I'm not angry with you," she said, sounding calmer now. "I'm angry at myself. Why don't I know what my unicorn magic is yet?!"

As Lei's eyes filled with tears, Isabelle sat down the other side of her and gave her a hug. "I'm sure you will soon," she told her cousin.

"But we've been too busy to go to Blossom Wood for a whole week – and now we're on this stupid nature walk!"

The three cousins had an incredible secret. At the start of their holiday together, they had found hoof prints in a cove near their campsite. When they'd stepped into them, they'd been

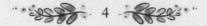

transported to an amazing land called
Blossom Wood, filled with animals.
What's more, in Blossom Wood, they
were no longer girls but unicorns!

"The walk isn't that bad," Isabelle said.
"Some of the birds we've spotted have
been really pretty."

"Yeah, but not as pretty as the ones in
Blossom Wood!" argued Lei. "And it's

OK for you – you know your unicorn magic is light. And Cora's is healing. What if I don't have any magic at all?" She buried her face in her hands, tipping her long hair forward and revealing the pink hair braids underneath. She hadn't been allowed to dye her hair pink like her older sister, so this was the next best thing!

"There's no way that we both have magic and you don't," Cora told her cousin. "You just have to be patient."

Above Lei's head, Isabelle raised her eyebrows at Cora. Lei was the least patient out of the three of them. In fact, she was the least patient person Isabelle knew! She jumped up, deciding the best thing to do was to try to take Lei's mind off it.

"Come on – I saw a pond up ahead,

with loads of tiny things growing in it.
Did you bring your microscope?"

Lei looked up, her face brighter now,
and she let Isabelle pull her from the
ground. "You bet!"

The three cousins clambered back over
the wall, and Isabelle pointed to the
pond in the distance.

Lei began sprinting towards it. "Last one there is a rotten egg!" she yelled.

"How much more cheese should I grate?" Isabelle asked Cora. Cora's blue eyes were filled with tears — but since

she was smiling, Isabelle guessed it was only from the onions she was peeling!

Cora looked at the pile of cheese, towering up from the chopping board like an Egyptian pyramid. "Um, unless you're planning to feed the whole campsite, I think that is enough!"

Isabelle grinned. "What? You can never have enough cheese!"

"Where's Lei got to?" Cora wondered, wiping away her onion tears and looking around. "She's been washing those peppers for ages."

The two girls glanced at each other. "Uh-oh!" they chorused, guessing exactly where she might be.

Isabelle thought quickly. "We're just going to the loo," she said to her mum, who was pulling the picnic plates out of a big basket.

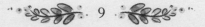

Cora's dad looked up from the ground, where he was lighting the cooking stove. "Both of you?"

Cora's mum nudged him. "Don't you know girls always like to go to the bathroom together?"

"It's where all the best gossiping happens!" Isabelle's mum added with a smile.

"Fair dinkum," Cora's dad said distractedly, then clapped his hands together – the stove was finally alight."

"Camping nachos are coming right up – so don't be long!"

"We won't!" Cora replied, already linking arms with Isabelle and running off.

"What's 'fair dinkum'?!" Isabelle asked as they jogged along. Although Cora's mum was English, Cora's dad was Australian, and he sometimes used words Isabelle had never heard of before!

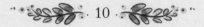

"It means real, or true," Cora explained. "Dad uses it a lot!"

They headed towards the toilet block, passing the washing-up station — where, as they'd guessed, Lei was nowhere to be seen. A bag of red and green peppers sat on the draining board, abandoned.

"I think we were right," said Isabelle, spotting the peppers. "We have to get to the cove!"

They veered off past the toilets to the edge of the Hilltop Hideaway campsite, then ran down the hill towards the small lake in the distance.

"Do you really think she would have gone there without us?" Cora panted.

"I don't know," Isabelle replied, her red, curly hair bouncing as they ran. "Maybe. You know what she's like..."

Cora nodded. Her cousin was a lot

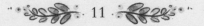

more confident and headstrong than she was. Once, Lei had even flown from her home in America all the way to London by herself, so she could stay with Isabelle for the Easter holidays while her parents were busy working. Still, going to Blossom Wood without them? Lei would have to be *really* upset to do that.

They reached the shore of the lake, where a family of swans were floating gracefully. Sand flew up from the girls' trainers as they sprinted towards the cove that was set into the hillside.

Isabelle squinted, trying to see into the shadows despite the bright sunshine. There was no sign of their cousin. "She must have gone!" she cried. "Quick, Cora, we have to go after her!"

But as they ducked into the cove and their eyes got used to the dark, they

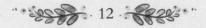

spotted a familiar figure curled up in
a corner.

"Lei, you're still here!" Cora rushed
over to her. "We thought you'd gone to
Blossom Wood."

Lei looked up, her face streaked with tears.
"I tried," she sniffed. "But it didn't work. I
don't think I have any magic left at all!"

Isabelle frowned. "That's weird. Why would it suddenly stop working?"

Cora stared at the three sets of hoof prints, deep in thought. "Maybe it only works if all three of us do it at the same time? We've never gone there separately before."

"No – it's me. It's all my fault!" Lei said uncertainly.

"Well," said Isabelle, stepping into one of the sets, "there's only one way to find out!"

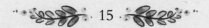

Chapter 2

Badger Falls

Cora and Lei jumped into the other sets of hoof prints beside Isabelle. Immediately, a warm, tingly feeling spread into their feet, legs and bodies.

"It's working!" shouted Lei as light flashed around them and she had to shut her eyes. Lei wanted to jump up and down in relief but decided she'd better keep her feet where they were. Her skin fizzed with magic and her head felt light and dreamy.

As the brightness faded, Lei opened her eyes again. "We're here!" she said, kicking up her front legs in excitement.

She trotted around, beaming at the sight of her two cousins – once again

beautiful, sleek white unicorns. Cora
was the tallest, like a racehorse, with a
flowing golden mane and tail. Isabelle
was a little smaller, with a curly red
mane. Lei flicked her own pink mane
around, neighing in excitement – they
were back in Blossom Wood!

As usual, they had arrived on a
mountain, near the hoof prints in the
ground that would take them back to
the cove whenever they wanted. Blossom
Wood spread out below them – the
cousins could see lush green trees,
shimmering glades and stunning flowers.
The Rushing River and Willow Lake
sparkled in the bright sunshine and there
were just a few fluffy white clouds in the
sky. From the look of the heat ripples
in the air, it had to be summer. It was
summer at home too, but the seasons

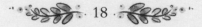

weren't always the same in both places —
when they'd been here last week, it had
been midwinter, and Blossom Wood was
covered in snow!

Cora backed into the shadows of the
mountain, golden sparks flying from
her hooves as they always did when
they hit the ground. It was part of her
magic. "Holy dooley — it's really hot here
today!"

Lei trotted to the edge of the
mountainside. The sparkles from her
hooves were pink, matching her mane
and tail. She looked around and asked,
"Where is everyone?"

The paths were mostly empty, but
Isabelle was nodding to the pool below
the waterfall that poured down the side
of the mountain. "I think they're all
cooling down!"

Lei followed her gaze and spotted animals of all kinds floating around in the water. "That looks awesome!" She began cantering down the mountain path, her pink tail swishing from side to side.

"Wait for us!" cried Isabelle. She galloped after her, red sparks shooting up as she raced along, enjoying the powerful feeling in her legs and body once more.

Cora stepped out of

the shadows and followed her cousins. She had expected to feel hot straight away, especially now the clouds had cleared from the sky completely, but although the sun shone down, she was nice and cool. The same thing had happened in the snow — she hadn't felt very cold, even when they'd trotted through thick snowdrifts. *Maybe it's because we're magic*, she wondered, then thought about what Lei had said. What if her cousin really didn't have magic like she and Isabelle did? Lei would never get over it!

As they neared the bottom of the mountain path, Cora pricked up her ears. She could hear shouts of laughter between splashes and giggles.

"Bobby!" Lei cantered over to their badger friend, who sat at the edge of the pool below the waterfall, his paws dangling in the water.

He turned, and a beam spread across his stripy face. "Unicorns! It's so lovely to see you!" He patted the bank beside him. "Come along now and cool off with us."

The other badgers, foxes, rabbits and squirrels in the water all waved as the unicorns trotted over to the pool.

Isabelle dipped a front hoof in the water. "That does feel

good," she said, easing forward until her whole body plunged in, sending splashes everywhere.

Cora laughed at Isabelle as she did a sort of doggy-paddle around the pool.

Loulou darted up behind them. The squirrel held an acorn cup in each paw, overflowing with pink liquid. "Would you like a refreshing peach punch?" she asked Lei and Cora, setting the drinks on the ground for the unicorns to sip.

"Mmmm, thank you." Cora shut her eyes as she savoured the sweet, fizzy drink, wondering if she could make it for herself back at home.

Lei neighed. "It's yummy!"

Cora smiled at her cousin. *At least she's in a better mood now*, she thought, *even if she still doesn't know what her magic is.*

"What's Isabelle doing?" asked Lei,

nodding to the other side of the pool. Isabelle looked like she was prancing in place, but in the water, sending red sparks the colour of her mane into the pool.

Bobby clapped his paws together. "It's her magic, I think?"

Sure enough, the red sparkles began to surround her body, head and horn, and soon light shimmered around Isabelle, making her look like a unicorn-shaped lantern.

Suddenly a duck shot up from beneath the water. "I've found it!" he yelled as he flapped on to the grassy bank clutching a reed ring in his webbed foot. "Thank treetops for that. My wife would have been furious if I'd lost my wedding ring!"

"Isabelle used her light to help the duck to see underwater," Cora realized. "Well done, Isabelle!"

Isabelle gave a deep nicker, then got back to swimming. Cora noticed a couple of worms taking a ride on her head as she swam, and giggled.

Alongside Bobby, Lei and Cora dipped their hooves in the cool pool, watching animals and insects play in the water.

They made Cora think of *The Wind in the Willows*, a book she'd recently read. Cora loved reading, especially when books took her on amazing, wonderful adventures just through her imagination. Although visiting Blossom Wood for real was the best adventure of all!

Lei felt a tiny tap on her front paw. She looked down and saw it was Wilf, a caterpillar.

"Hi, unicorns! It's brilliant to see you! Are you enjoying the sunny weather? Will you take a dip? I can't swim, unfortunately, but I don't mind — it's fun just watching everyone, don't you think?"

"Hey, Wilf," Lei said to the chatty creature. "Yeah, I might go for a swim soon."

"Wasn't it great, what Isabelle did in the water with her magic?" Wilf

continued, then he nodded at Cora. "So if Cora's magic is healing, and Isabelle can create light, what's yours, Lei?"

Lei rose up on her hind legs and pawed the air, making everyone around her jump with fright. "I don't know!" she yelled, dropping her front hooves back to the ground in a fizz of pink sparks.

"Maybe I don't have any magic at all!"

"I'm sorry," said Wilf, waving his little legs madly in apology. "I was just being friendly. I didn't mean to make you angry."

Lei didn't reply, but spun around and galloped back towards the mountain path instead, sparkles flying from her hooves.

"It's not your fault," Cora whispered to Wilf, while thinking, *So I was wrong about Lei being in a better mood!* "She's been upset about it all day."

Bobby pulled a sympathetic face. "Oh dear, poor Lei. But she just has to be patient. It'll come, I'm sure."

Cora was about to tell Bobby that patience wasn't one of Lei's strong points when thunder rumbled above.

Wilf looked up. "Where did those black clouds come from?" The angry clouds were rushing in across the sky,

and suddenly everything was in gloom.

As rain began to hammer down, making dimples on the water, Isabelle trotted out of the pool. Everyone was taking shelter, except for the frogs and worms, who were jumping and sliding about. Isabelle smiled at them – they looked like they loved the rain.

Cora nudged Isabelle to one side and explained what had happened with Lei.

"We should follow her," Cora said. "If she wants to go home, she won't be able to do it without us."

"If the weather's turning bad, we should probably go back anyway," Isabelle replied.

Cora nodded and called, "Hooroo, Bobby," which Isabelle was pretty sure meant goodbye in Australia. "We'd better go after Lei."

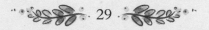

"I understand," he said, waving and then ducking into his nearby badger sett to get out of the rain.

"Lei. LEI! Wait for us!" Isabelle shouted over the thunder as they galloped

up the mountain, rain pouring down
her already wet back. As the shortest
unicorn – she was the size of a pony,
really – Lei was the slowest. This was
lucky, as it meant they could catch
her up, their hooves pounding the wet
ground, red and golden sparks flashing
around them. Soon they could see their
friend at the bend of the mountain
path ahead.

Lei didn't stop at first, but then
different yells rang out behind the
unicorns.

"Wait! Unicorns! We need your
help!"

Now Lei skidded to a halt. She spun
around, her brown eyes widened and
she began racing back down the
rocky path.

Isabelle and Cora turned in the

direction of the shouts, and saw two bright-purple frogs hopping madly towards them, looking very worried indeed.

Chapter 3

The Storm

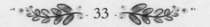

"Whatever's the matter?" Isabelle asked, lowering her head to hear the frogs over the crashing raindrops.

"It's the storm!" the biggest frog told them.

"It's flooding Blossom Wood," the other one explained. "Can you help?"

"Sure – we have to!" said Lei, panting.

"I saw it after you called — from higher up the mountain. It looks pretty bad!"

Isabelle bent her head down further so the frogs could leap on to her red forelock and ride between her ears. "Come on — it'll be quicker if you take a ride."

The unicorns began galloping back down the mountain, with the frogs riding on Isabelle, holding on to her red mane.

"Head to Willow Lake," one croaked. "It's worst there."

They passed Badger Falls, where the waterfall crashed madly down into the pool. It reminded Lei of the holiday when they'd all visited Niagara Falls.

"How come everywhere's flooding so quickly?" Cora asked as they bolted along.

"It's because it's been so hot," Lei explained. "It's called flash flooding. The ground is too hard to soak up the water because it's been baked by the sun."

"That makes sense," Cora replied. "You know so much about science!"

"So how can we stop it?" Isabelle panted.

Lei shook her head, sending droplets from her sodden pink mane flying. "We can't −

we just have to hope the rain stops!"

The silver willow trees around Willow Lake drooped heavily in the pouring rain, creating a thick wet curtain. The unicorns stuck their muzzles through it, and gasped at the sight. Ducks and other birds were flying around in panic, while frogs and toads leapt across the lily pads, carrying belongings from their homes.

Lei rushed to the edge of the water. "We've got to help them get to safety!"

"I'll help the frogs and toads," Isabelle offered.

"And I'll go see the ducks," said Cora. "They look like they need some calming down."

Lei neighed and nodded. "I'll go and give those beavers over there some help." She could see four of them struggling in the rising water as they tried to leave

their wooden home, which was built into the side of the lake.

Soon, all of the bigger animals were helping the smaller ones get somewhere dry. As Lei used her hooves to pull the beavers to safety, she spotted a bear carrying three tortoises in its big paws, and two deer swimming across Willow Lake to rescue a baby otter who'd got separated from his family. The otters could stay in the water, of course, but the flooding was making huge waves, and the otters needed to stay away from the powerful currents in the Rushing River, which linked to Willow Lake.

"The whole forest is flooding!" yelled Cora as she carried the ducks away from their submerged reed home. She was wading through water up to her chest,

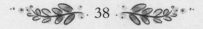

and couldn't see anywhere dry to set them down.

"We can fly from here," quacked a duck who'd introduced herself as Hampton. "And we can go and make shelters in the trees for any animal who needs it."

"Great idea!" replied Monty – the duck who'd lost his wedding ring in the pool. They fluttered up off Cora's back, into the rain, which showed no sign of stopping.

"The rabbits!" cried Isabelle, as she spotted a whole family of bunnies splashing out of their burrow not far from Willow Lake. She recognized one of them as Lizzie, the rabbit they'd rescued from a cave the last time they'd been here – and there was Billy too, Lizzie's brother. "Jump on!" she told them, lowering her head

once more, and they scampered up to settle themselves on her glossy white back.

"Hold on to my mane," she told them. "It's slippery up there!"

Isabelle trotted slowly away from the lake, in the direction the ducks flew. The Moon Chestnut tree rose up ahead of her – it was the tallest tree in the wood, and shaped like a crescent moon. The woodlanders believed it was magical, because it was the oldest tree in the forest.

By the time she reached it, the floodwater was sloshing around the tree and splashing on to Isabelle's body as she moved. She spotted Hampton and Monty on a branch above her head, placing twigs into the crook where it met the trunk.

"Rabbits, you'll be safe here!" quacked

Hampton, waving a wing to beckon them up.

Isabelle raised her head up to the branch so the bunnies could scamper from her back to her head to jump off to their temporary home.

"Thank you, thank you!" squeaked Billy, waving a paw from the dry branch. "You saved us."

"And you saved me again!" added Lizzie. "I owe you a big dandelion pie."

With a neigh of thanks, Isabelle turned to go back to the lake. Cora and Lei were cantering towards her, carrying beavers on their backs.

"Is there room for them in the Moon Chestnut?" Cora asked the ducks, who were busily making more new homes higher up the tree.

"Yes!" Monty replied. "Send 'em up!"

The beavers hugged Cora and Lei before jumping off on to branches of the

towering chestnut tree.

Isabelle whinnied as relief spread a warm glow through her. *We can do this!* she thought as she saw more and more animals being carried to safety by bigger creatures and lifted up into the trees around them. She looked up at the charcoal-grey sky, still hammering giant raindrops down on Blossom Wood. *I just wish it would stop raining!*

A splash below her made Isabelle look down. At first, all she could see was a little black nose peeping up from the water, but then she caught sight of white stripes. . .

"Bobby!" she realized. "What are you doing?!"

The badger splashed over to the Moon Chestnut's trunk and clung on with his claws. "I had to come. I didn't know

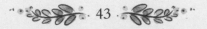

what else to do, you see. Badger Falls is
flooding!"

Chapter 4

The Rescue

Lei snorted with worry. "Your home!" she cried.

Bobby nodded. "I'm afraid the pool around the waterfall has burst its banks, and the water's heading straight to our badger homes under the ground. Can you help?"

"Of course!" yelled the three unicorns

together. They began wading through the water, Bobby swimming after them in his funny style that was more splashing than a proper swimming stroke.

"I didn't know badgers could swim," said Cora.

"We can, but I'd really prefer not to!" Bobby panted, paws splashing everywhere.

"You should have said!" Lei told him. "Come up on to my back." As the shortest of the unicorns, Lei's back

was only just above the water, making it easy for Bobby to climb up her pink tail and on to her back.

"I haven't done this much exercise in a long time," Bobby said breathlessly. "But I had to get help – everyone else is trying to stop the flooding."

Lei, Cora and Isabelle pushed through the water, cantering when it was low enough, swimming when it got too high. They passed apple trees and pine trees, chestnut trees and oak trees, the branches all filled with animals escaping the floods.

"Here we are!" Bobby growled deeply as they moved on to an area of earthy ground in front of Badger Falls. "We didn't think it would flood here, because it's a bit higher, but it looks like nothing is stopping this storm!"

He lumbered over to his own sett, peering down the tunnel leading to it. "Oh chestnuts, the water's getting in. Oh, my rugs! My candles!"

"At least you're OK," said Isabelle. "That's the main thing. But I think we need to evacuate all the badgers too."

"You're right," Lei said with a neigh. "Let's get everyone out of their setts and up the mountain."

They began looking into badger tunnels and calling the animals out as quickly as possible.

"Why in Blossom Wood did the weather change so quickly today?" Bobby wondered to himself as he pointed a family of dripping badgers in the direction of the mountain path. "Hot sunshine one moment, a terrible storm the next." He wiped his eyes clear of the

rain. "That never happens here. Maybe it's magic. Or just bad luck. Whatever it is, I don't like it."

Lei's ears pricked up at Bobby's mention of magic. It was the first time she'd thought about magic since the storm had started, and she remembered her anger about not having a magical power. She thought back to the weather she'd seen in Blossom Wood ever since the first time they came – the thunder and lightning out of the blue, the snow blizzard, and today's freak storm. Could it be something to do with the unicorns? Could it be something to do with *her*?

Lei shook her head quickly, as if to shake the thought away. *Don't be stupid*, she told herself. She was just jumping to conclusions. She continued peeking into the badger setts, her mind soon focused

on helping a young badger and his father out of a particularly long tunnel with her hoof.

As a baby badger scampered out of a hole, Cora held out a leg. "Climb up on me, so you don't get too wet," she suggested.

"Oh, thank you," said the baby's mother behind her. "She's too big for me to carry, and too scared to walk herself. I didn't know how I was going to get her up the mountain!"

As she listened to the badger, Lei felt hot with guilt — the storm was making everyone so unhappy! She pushed the bad feeling away and kept going, finding a couple of mice she recognized in a tiny hole. Mo and May grabbed Lei's tail, and she trotted up the path until she could drop them off in a place without any puddles.

"Thank you!" they squeaked as they scurried further up the mountain.

"That's everyone!" Bobby announced as Lei arrived back at Badger Falls.

"Thank treetops," Isabelle replied, using the saying she'd heard Bobby use.

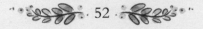

She'd been writing everything she could remember down in her diary back at the tent, including Bobby's sayings. Once their holiday had finished, she didn't want to forget a moment of it — and she thought she might even try to write a Blossom Wood story.

They'd got everyone out in the nick of time. Water from the pool they'd been swimming in just a little while ago was pouring into the badgers' tunnels now — it wouldn't have been safe inside them.

"Let's check they've found somewhere to shelter up the mountain," Cora suggested, and began trotting up it, shaking her soaking golden mane, which was weighed down with rain.

Bobby glanced at his home and shook his head sadly. "Oh, I do hope

 53

everything isn't ruined." Then he bent
his head back to look at the sky and said
to it, "Please stop now! Please!"

His words stabbed at Lei's heart like needles. She couldn't keep her worries inside any longer. "It's not the sky, Bobby. I think it's me!"

Chapter 5

Lei's Magic

"What in Blossom Wood are you talking about?" asked Isabelle, using another of Bobby's phrases.

Cora stopped trotting up the mountain, turned around and frowned. "How can it be you?"

Lei lowered her head in shame and spoke in a whisper. "I think it might be my magic. The weather's only been weird since we've been here. The thunder, the snow, the storm. And it seems to happen when I'm angry – when I stomp my hooves."

Isabelle's green eyes widened. "Oh no ... it can't be."

Cora looked up at the still-grey sky, her mind racing with thoughts. "It *does* make sense," she said eventually. "But the only way to know for certain is to try it out..."

"I can't do that!" said Lei. "Look what I've done already!"

With a splash, Bobby put a paw on Lei's hoof. "Well, the weather can't really get any worse, can it now? I think you should try."

Lei took a long, deep breath. "OK," she said, puffing out slowly. "If you're sure?"

Bobby, Cora and Isabelle all nodded as the rain continued to hammer down around them.

Lei trotted along the mountain path and the others followed, until she found a dry patch under an overhang in the shadows of the mountain. Then she began prancing in place. Lei focused on the pink sparks shooting up from the ground and began trotting in circles, feeling the warmth in her hooves spread to her legs and her body. The sparks felt tingly as she kept moving, and started to fizz across her back and her chest before sparkling around her head.

"Keep going!" shouted Isabelle.

Cora neighed. "You can do it!" she added.

Still trotting, Lei felt hot with magic now, and she began to think of the

weather. As pink sparks shot around her head and out from her horn, she pointed it to the sky and thought only of good weather. *Stop raining*, she said in her mind. *Rain, rain, go away, and let summer come back to Blossom Wood!*

Her pink sparkles began spinning out of her horn and up into the sky like a glittery party popper. Lei felt the warmth in her fade away, and with it the magic. She watched the sky, waiting for the rain to stop.

It didn't. The clouds were as grey as ever. The storm kept hammering down across Blossom Wood.

"It hasn't worked!" Lei cried, not knowing whether to feel pleased or disappointed. She was glad it hadn't been her who caused the awful weather, but she had so wanted to stop it – and if *that* wasn't her magic, then what was it? She was back to square one!

Cora and Isabelle trotted to Lei's side, and nudged their heads to hers to comfort their cousin.

"I'm sorry," Cora whispered.

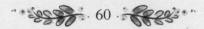

Isabelle nickered. "I'm sure you'll find out what your magic is soon."

Lei shook her head. "You're always so positive," she said to Isabelle. "But I'm just going to have to get used to the fact that I'm a unicorn without any magic ... It sucks that I can't help!"

Bobby put a hand on his hip. "Don't forget my Auntie Bina's story." The first time the unicorns had met Bobby, he'd told them his auntie's tale of how

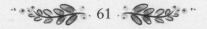

unicorns were extremely special. The legend said that they weren't only magical, but that every unicorn had a different kind of magic to help the woodland creatures in different ways. "Now I've met you, I believe what Auntie Bina told me was real, and not just a story."

"Thanks, Bobby. But you said yourself that you're not sure how much of the legend is true. Maybe only *some* unicorns are magical."

Cora only half heard what Lei was saying. She'd noticed something in the sky: a patch of blue, far in the distance. "LOOK!" she shouted, her head high.

The others followed her gaze.

"Oh treetops!" Bobby ran down the hill and raised his paws to the sky. The

dark clouds were clearing, right in front
of their eyes.

Isabelle pointed her horn upwards.
"The rain – it's stopping." She turned to

Lei. "You did it — YOU DID IT!"

Lei scanned the sky, watching a big grey cloud float away to reveal the sun peeking out behind it. "Are you sure?" she asked.

"Deffo!" Cora kicked up her front hooves. "There's no way the weather could have changed that quickly — unless it was magic!" Cora beamed. Before they'd first visited Blossom Wood, she hadn't even believed in magic, but now she did. She'd never been more certain of anything!

Lei pranced in place, warm tingles of happiness shooting through her now, replacing the warm magic of moments ago. "This is amazing!" she neighed.

Then she stopped suddenly.

"What's wrong?" Isabelle asked.

"This isn't amazing at all. It sucks!"

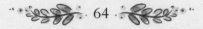

Lei said, her brown eyes welling up
with tears.

"What do you mean?" Bobby asked in
his gravelly voice.

"I caused the storm — and I caused the
flooding," Lei explained. "It was all my
fault!"

Bobby patted Lei's hoof again. "Don't
be silly. It wasn't your fault, not at
all. You had
absolutely no idea
what your magic
was!"

Cora felt bad
for her cousin —
she understood
why she felt

guilty — but agreed with Bobby completely. "You didn't know, so you can't blame yourself. And you fixed it!"

"And anyway," added Isabelle, "now you know what your magic is, you can make sure the weather is never bad again. That's a brilliant power!"

Lei shrugged. "Maybe..." She tried to feel happy, but to her, Isabelle's magic of light and Cora's ability to heal seemed a lot better. Prickles of envy filled her chest.

"Well, I for one think controlling the weather is extremely special," said Bobby. "It's so big and powerful and important. We will need you just as much as we need Cora and Isabelle. I'm sure of it."

Isabelle's mind buzzed with an idea. "Does it mean that you can summon any sort of weather you want?"

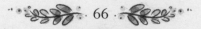

"Um, I guess," said Lei.

"So can we have rainbows?" Isabelle asked.

Cora flicked her tail and widened her blue eyes pleadingly. "Oh yes – go on, Lei. Can you see if you can do it?"

Chapter 6

The Rainbow Party!

Everyone was being so nice to her, Lei felt she had to try. *And anyway,* she thought, *creating rainbows would be pretty awesome!*

Now it was no longer raining, she trotted out of the shelter of the mountain. To her relief, Lei could see that the floodwater was already receding, and creatures were starting to flutter about the wood once more. She could hear all sorts of birds tweeting their beautiful songs again as she began stamping every one of her four hooves on the rocky ground.

"Here goes," she said, trotting in circles in front of Isabelle, Cora and Bobby. Pink sparks flew up like the crackles from a fire, and Lei felt the magical warmth spread through her hooves, legs and body. As she fizzed with magic, she thought only of rainbows, imagining hundreds of them across the now-blue Blossom Wood sky.

Cora watched Lei carefully, trying not to worry about how her cousin would react if it didn't work. But something was definitely happening – Lei was so surrounded by sparkles, she looked like a glittery Christmas card!

As Lei felt the magic gather in her horn, she stared at the sky. *Rainbows, rainbows, rainbows!* she thought as the sparkles shot out of her horn and upwards. She only lowered her head again when she felt the magic and warmth disappear.

The three unicorns and badger waited, not talking and not even blinking as they stared upwards.

Isabelle crossed her front hooves hopefully. *Come on, it has to work!* she told herself.

Lei was just about to ask how long they should wait, when she spotted something above Willow Lake. A flash of colours: red, orange, yellow, green, blue, indigo and violet.

"A rainbow!" she cried, prancing on the spot and sending more pink sparks shooting up from the ground. "It IS my magic!"

Cora nudged Lei to get her attention. "Wait – look!"

Lei looked around and saw what Cora had spotted: another rainbow, starting at the peak of one of the mountains. Lei

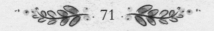

opened her mouth to speak, but nothing would come out.

"That's the first time I've seen you speechless," Isabelle joked with a grin.

Meanwhile, Bobby was bouncing around beside them, pointing upwards. "There are rainbows EVERYWHERE!"

It was true – they were flashing up all over Blossom Wood as if someone was painting them into the sky.

"I did this," Lei finally whispered, still staring at the gorgeous rainbows above her. "I did this!"

"What's that noise?" asked Cora, moving her ears forward to catch it properly. "It sounds like cheering."

Bobby nodded. "I may be older than I'd like to admit, but there's nothing wrong with my hearing. It IS cheering."

As they looked around Blossom Wood

from their position partway up the mountain, they spotted animals of every kind clapping and pointing at the sky.

"Everyone's REALLY happy about the rainbows," said Cora, a bit surprised at just how excited all the woodlanders seemed.

Then a small brown bird shot past, tweeting at them over her shoulder, "RAINBOW PARTY!"

Bobby laughed. "I was wondering who'd be the first to say that. We need to gather all the woodlanders to celebrate! Winnie, can you spread the word?" he called after the cute little bird. Winnie nodded and grinned as she flew off.

Lei frowned. "What do you mean?"

"What's a rainbow party?" Isabelle asked, although she already knew she wanted to go to one. Just the name sounded brilliant.

Bobby raised his bushy black eyebrows in surprise. "You mean you haven't been to a rainbow party before? Well, you're in for a treat, I must say. Come – follow me."

They trotted after Bobby down the mountainside. At the bottom of the path, the water was just shallow puddles now – it looked like the flood was drying up quickly. Lei sighed deeply with relief.

"Where are we going?" Isabelle asked Bobby. "What happens at the party?"

Bobby smiled and kept walking. "You'll have to wait and see. I promise it'll be worth it!"

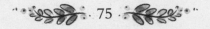

They followed a woodland path through the Oval of Oaks. Cora spotted the Moon Chestnut tree in the distance. It looked a lot different from the last time she'd seen it – now it wasn't surrounded by floodwater. Instead, it was swarmed by woodland creatures of every kind!

"I must leave you for a moment," Bobby told them as they reached the crowd of animals. "I won't be long."

Lei looked at Cora and Isabelle. "What's going to happen?"

Cora shrugged. "I guess we'll just have to wait and see!"

The badger reached the Moon Chestnut's trunk and stood on one of its raised roots to see over the crowd. He clapped his paws together and coughed loudly. "Ahem. Ahem! Before we begin this rainbow party, I just want to say a

few words. As you all know, rainbows are incredibly rare and special, which is why we always try to have a rainbow party when one appears. But today it's extra special, because there are too many rainbows in the sky to count! Today, Lei has discovered her unicorn power – to change the weather. What a wonderful thing!"

Bobby's words were drowned out as all the woodlanders clapped and cheered, turning to Lei and staring at her in awe.

Lei felt her cheeks go hot with embarrassment, and was glad when Bobby started asking for everyone's attention again.

"What's more," the badger continued, "it turns out that our unicorns here have never been to a rainbow party, so let's make it the best one yet!"

A duck band – the same one that'd

played at the midwinter festival –
immediately started up, and the creatures
formed several circles around the
gigantic Moon
Chestnut tree.

"Come on!" said Isabelle, nudging her cousins and flicking her tail to the music. The unicorns joined one of the circles and began to dance around the tree to the beats of the ducks' drumming. As pink, red and golden sparks flew from their hooves, the unicorns made sure they copied everyone else so they didn't go the wrong way.

"Let's all do the Rainbow Dance, let's all do the Rainbow Dance," everyone began to sing, while Bobby stayed in the middle by the tree trunk, beaming as he watched the animals flicking up their hooves, paws and tails and swaying to the music. Multicoloured light shone down from the hundreds of rainbows in the sky, making everyone glow in red, orange, yellow, green, blue, indigo and violet. Now, not just the sky but the

whole of Blossom Wood was covered in rainbows!

As she danced, Lei's mind raced with everything that'd happened that day. She still felt a little guilty about causing the flood, but the woodlanders seemed so happy about her weather magic that it didn't feel right to be sad. And she knew she'd only use it for good in the future. From the delighted looks on everyone's faces at the sight of all the rainbows, maybe her magic *was* just as special as Isabelle's and Cora's, Lei decided.

After several songs, the duck band paused, calling for a short break, although the rainbows still shone brightly above them. "We'll be right back!" Monty assured everyone.

Bobby padded over to the unicorns,

waving to get their attention. "Are you enjoying the party?"

Isabelle whinnied loudly. "You were right, Bobby, it was worth waiting for," she said, flicking her red tail around the badger in a hug.

Lei nickered and bent her head down to Bobby. "Thank you. This is amazing," she told him.

Bobby put his paws out towards the unicorn and kissed her nose. "No, thank YOU," he said, "for bringing so much joy to Blossom Wood. It certainly has been a day to remember."

All three unicorns neighed back as one. They couldn't argue with that!

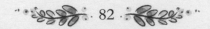

Did You Know?

❀ As Lei mentions in the story, flash flooding happens when a lot of rain falls after a long period of dry weather. If the ground is hard, it is unable to soak up the water which causes the flooding.

❀ There is a tribe of people called the Korowai tribe who build their houses in trees to avoid them becoming flooded. These treehouses can be built as high as 35 metres off the ground – that's 3 metres higher than the top of the Tower of London.

❀ A rainbow is caused when we see the sun's light through rain or other droplets of water in the air. The seven colours that you can see in a rainbow are red, orange, yellow, green, blue, indigo and violet.

Spot the Difference

Can you spot five things that are different in these pictures?

Spot the Difference Answers

Lei Fact File

Lei discovers her weather magic in this story. Here are some more fun facts about Lei.

Name: Lei Sutton

Age: 9

Family: Lives with her mum, dad and sister, Ying

Home Town: San Francisco, California, United States of America

Pets: A horse called Duke

Favourite drink: Peach soda

Favourite book: *The Everything Kids' Science*

Experiments Book by Tom Robinson

Favourite word: Awesome

Likes: Doing science experiments, riding her horse, cooking

Dislikes: Being left behind

Unicorn Pairs

Can you match each girl with their unicorn forms?

Unicorns to the Rescue!

Can you help Cora, Lei and Isabelle rescue
Bobby from the water? Pick the path that will
lead them to his side.

Start

Try Again!

Finish

Try Again!

Word Search

Can you find five trees that grow in Blossom Wood in this word search?

X	B	O	V	W	T	A	R	Y	U
O	R	P	I	N	E	N	L	J	W
E	Z	Y	A	E	Q	T	S	O	I
A	V	S	C	H	X	Y	I	L	L
C	H	E	S	T	N	U	T	M	L
S	Z	I	A	F	D	T	Y	B	L
N	A	H	Z	W	A	S	Y	I	O
Q	O	X	A	P	P	L	E	U	W
Z	A	J	H	S	P	Y	O	H	D
V	K	A	U	G	K	L	X	Z	S

❀ Chestnut ❀ Pine ❀ Willow

❀ Oak ❀ Apple

Meet

The Owls of Blossom Wood

in these magical books

Turn over for a sneak peek of another The Unicorns of Blossom Wood adventure!

Catherine Coe

Unicorn games & quizzes inside!

The Unicorns of Blossom Wood
❋ Best Friends ❋

Chapter 2
Bobby the Magician

Isabelle's whole body fizzed and tingled and fizzed some more. She still had her eyes tight shut, but the bright light was disappearing now. She slowly opened them ... and gasped at the view. Even though this was her fourth time in Blossom Wood, its beauty still took her breath away. She looked down on trees in every shade of green, the leaves twinkling in the sunlight. Perfect fluffy white clouds dotted the turquoise-blue sky, and Willow Lake shone like a jewel in the distance. As usual, they'd arrived high up on a mountain, and could see the whole stunning wood stretched out beneath them.

Isabelle turned to her cousins and neighed excitedly. They were no longer girls, but unicorns again! The sight of their glossy white coats and shiny manes made Isabelle toss her own red mane in delight.

Cora blinked her blue eyes, as if she couldn't quite believe it. "We're back!" She trotted carefully out of the hoof prints that would take them home again when they were ready. As she neared the edge of the mountain, she smiled at the

powerful feeling in her unicorn legs. Cora was the biggest of the three – the size of a racehorse. She could gallop so fast everything she passed became a blur. "It looks really busy down there today..."

Lei squinted at the thick forests below. "Yeah, that's true," she said, noticing rabbits scampering and bees buzzing and birds fluttering all around. Willow Lake was filled with waves and splashes, and Foxglove Glade was crowded with creatures. "I wonder what's going on?"

Isabelle was already cantering down the rocky mountain path. "Let's go and see!" she said and whinnied, flicking her red tail as she raced along. Sparks flew from her hooves as they hit the ground – these were magical sparks, which gave Isabelle a special power. She could light up like a lantern in the dark!

Lei quickly followed her cousin, pink sparks fizzing from her own hooves to match her pink mane and tail. She'd only recently discovered her magical power – she could control the weather. But she didn't need to do anything about it today. The sunshine was warm but not too hot, and there was a gentle, refreshing breeze in the air. Lei galloped to catch up to Isabelle. She was the smallest of the unicorns, like a pony, which meant she had to work hard to move at the same speed as her cousins. Not that she minded – galloping as a unicorn was even better than riding her horse at home!

Behind them, Cora raced along. Her sparks were golden, and her magical power was healing, although she hoped she wouldn't have to use it today. Cora's

long, strong legs meant she quickly
caught up to Isabelle and Lei, and by
the time they reached the bottom of
the mountain, the three unicorns were
trotting alongside each other.